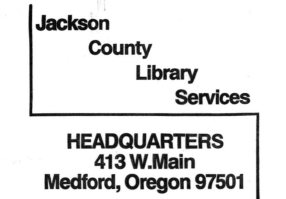

Chubbo's Pool

Written and illustrated by BETSY LEWIN

Clarion Books / *New York*

Clarion Books
a Houghton Mifflin Company imprint
215 Park Avenue South, New York, NY 10003
Text and illustrations copyright © 1996 by Betsy Lewin
The illustrations for this book were executed in watercolors on Strathmore 5-ply Bristol.
The text is set in 16/20-point Dante.

For information about permission to reproduce selections from this book, write to Permissions,
Houghton Mifflin Company, 215 Park Avenue South, New York, NY 10003.

For information about this and other Houghton Mifflin trade and reference books and multimedia products,
visit The Bookstore at Houghton Mifflin on the World Wide Web at (http://www.hmco.com/trade/).

Printed in the USA

Library of Congress Cataloging-in-Publication Data
Lewin, Betsy.
Chubbo's pool / written and illustrated by Betsy Lewin.
p.   cm.
Summary: A selfish hippopotamus, who will not share his pool with the other animals,
learns a lesson about cooperation and sharing.
ISBN 0-395-72807-X
[1. Hippopotamus—Fiction.   2. Animals—Fiction.   3. Sharing—Fiction.]   I. Title.
PZ7.L58417Ch   1997
[E]—dc20   95-20467
CIP
AC
HOR 10 9 8 7 6 5 4 3 2 1

To Sheila Youthed and Amadeus (the real "Chubbo")

On the hottest day ever, Chubbo found an empty pool. "Good," said Chubbo. "This pool is all mine."

He sank into the cool water
and blew bubbles through his nose.
He closed his eyes and grunted, "Wonk, wonk, wonk."

Chubbo sank deeper into the pool.
Only his little piggy ears showed on the surface.
He heard rustling grass and the footsteps
of zebras and warthogs coming to drink
and wallow in the mud at the edge of the pool.

Chubbo burst to the surface and bellowed,
"GET OUT OF MY POOL!"
The startled animals turned and fled
without getting even their hooves wet.

Chubbo had just settled himself back into his pool
when a chattering troop of thirsty baboons
made their way down to the water's edge.

"GET OUT OF MY POOL!" roared Chubbo.
The frightened troop bolted in all directions
without getting even a sip of water.

"GET OUT OF MY POOL!" Chubbo roared again,
when a family of elephants tried to share the pool.
All his thrashing churned up the muddy bottom of the pool.
The elephants fled, ears out, tails up, and still thirsty.

17

The days wore on and the sun beamed down.
Now there wasn't enough water for Chubbo himself.
Hot and thirsty, he set out to find another pool.

When he found one, it was full of animals.
There were the zebras and warthogs,
the baboon troop and the elephant family,
all sharing the pool with one another
and lots of other animals, too.
They didn't chase Chubbo away.
But they didn't invite him to join them, either.

Chubbo knew he wasn't welcome. He turned away
and trudged slowly back to his pool, which was now
only a mud wallow.

Chubbo was very hot, very thirsty,
and very, very alone.
Suddenly, Chubbo felt the ground beneath him
shake like an earthquake.

ELEPHANTS!

One by one they came, trunks curled,
and circled Chubbo's pool.
Then, "**WHOOSH!**" The pool was full of water again.

Chubbo sank into the cool water and grunted,
"Wonk, wonk, wonk."
He thought about how nice it was to have a pool,
and friends to share it with.

Author's Note

This is a fictional story inspired by my experience in Botswana's Okavango Delta with a real hippo who refused to share his part of the river with anyone else.

Animal Glossary

Elephant:
Loxodonta africana

Hippopotamus:
Hippopotamus amphibius

Southern Giraffe:
Giraffa camelopardalis giraffa

Waterbuck:
Kobus ellipsiprymus

Warthog:
Phacochoerus aethiopicus

Chacma Baboon:
Papio ursinus

Chapman's Zebra:
Equus burchelli antiquorum

Hamerkop:
Scopus umbretta umbretta

Cattle Egret:
Bubulcus ibis

Lappet-faced Vulture:
Torgos tracheliotus

Blacksmith Plover:
Hoplopterus armatus